Where's My T·R·U·C·K?

by **Karen Beaumont**

pictures by **David Catrow**

SCHOLASTIC INC.
New York Toronto London Auckland
Sydney Mexico City New Delhi Hong Kong

"**Shhh!**" I hear my parents say,
"Tommy's not himself today.
He's lost his **T·R·U·C·K!**"

My brother says, "Let's climb a tree."
My sister says, "Play house with me."
But all I want to do today
Is find my T·R·U·C·K!

I look behind my closet door.
I dig through every dresser drawer.

I search my brother's pile of junk.
I look in Grandma's smelly trunk.

And underneath the bed . . .

And chair.

Behind the curtain . . .
   OOPS! Not there!

I CANNOT FIND IT ANYWHERE!

My brother tosses me a ball.
My sister hands me some dumb doll.
My mom says it will be okay.
My dad just shrugs and walks away.

I WANT MY T·R·U·C·K!

I dump my toy box on the floor.
I look . . .
And look . . .
And look some more.

I've never lost my truck before.

I go outside . . .
Where could it be?
Is it underneath the tree?

In the sandbox?
By the shed?
Maybe in the
flower bed?

I climb
up on
the ladder . . .
Hey!

Is that my T·R·U·C·K?

I look again
but still
no luck.

Did someone
steal my
favorite truck?

I had my
red truck
yesterday.

A toy truck
can't just
drive away!

My brother hands me his green jeep.
My dad says I just need more sleep.
My sister says, "Come on. Let's play!"
My mom just whispers, "What a day."

I WANT MY T·R·U·C·K!

I don't want jeeps or cars or planes,
Or boats or bikes or trikes or trains.
I don't want green or blue or black.
I only want my red truck back.

I look once more out on the lawn.

MY T·R·U·C·K IS GONE!

I loved that truck.
I love it still.
I always, always, always will.

That truck hauled toys
and tools and rocks,
Banana peels and dirty socks,
Great big bones for Bowser . . .

Wait!
What's he doing
by the gate?

Bowser's dug a giant hole.
Something's buried by his bowl.
Something . . . kind of red . . .

HOORAY!

I FOUND MY T·R·U·C·K!

Come on, Bowser!

Let's go play!

With all my love to John,
who likes big trucks, fast cars,
and other toys that go vroom!
—KB

To Bob Alexander,
the first artist I ever knew.
—DC

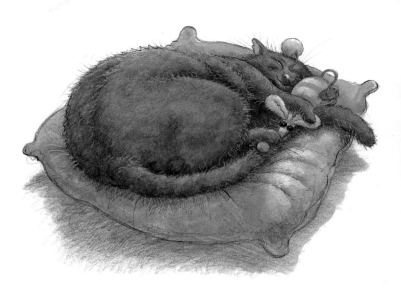

ISBN 978-0-545-48067-3

Text copyright © 2011 by Karen Beaumont.
Pictures copyright © 2011 by David Catrow.
All rights reserved. Published by Scholastic Inc.,
557 Broadway, New York, NY 10012,
by arrangement with Dial Books for Young Readers,
a division of Penguin Young Readers Group,
a member of Penguin Group (USA) Inc.
SCHOLASTIC and associated logos are trademarks
and/or registered trademarks of Scholastic Inc.

12 11 10 9 8 7 6 5 4 3 2 1   12 13 14 15 16 17/0

Printed in the U.S.A.   08

First Scholastic printing, September 2012

Designed by Lily Malcom
Text set in Slappy
The art was created using pencil and watercolor.